CW00848220

Tiberius
goes to London
A Longer Tiberius Tale

for Charlotte and Pru

First published by Tiberius Publishing
The Cottage
8 Kimberley Road
Nuthall
Nottingham NG16 1DG

Written by Keith Harvey
Designed and illustrated by Kait Brown

First published in 2004
Copyright © Tiberius Publishing

A CIP catalogue record for this title is available from the British Library.

Hardback ISBN: 1 902604 06 7
Printed and bound in Spain

10 9 8 7 6 5 4 3 2 1

Tiberius
goes to London
A Longer Tiberius Tale

Written by Keith Harvey

Illustrated by Kait Brown

Tiberius, a little mouse with pink ears and an extremely long tail, was waiting at his house for his friends to arrive. Sneaky Cat, Croaky Crow and Drag had agreed with Tiberius that they should all have a day out together.

Today they were going to choose where they were going.

Tiberius had got up early, had his breakfast and was just washing up when there was a loud knock at the door.

It made him jump so much he nearly dropped his cup and saucer.

'Who can that be?' he thought. 'It's only half past nine and I am not expecting anyone until 10 o'clock.'

Tiberius went to the door and opened it.

"Hi Tiberius," said Sneaky Cat. "I'm sorry I'm early. I have been so excited about planning a day out that I couldn't wait to get here."

"Not a problem," said Tiberius. "Come in."

"What are they?" asked Tiberius, pointing to some papers Sneaky was carrying.

"Oh, they're brochures," said Sneaky Cat, "but I will show them to you later when the others arrive."

When Drag and Croaky Crow arrived, they were also carrying brochures.

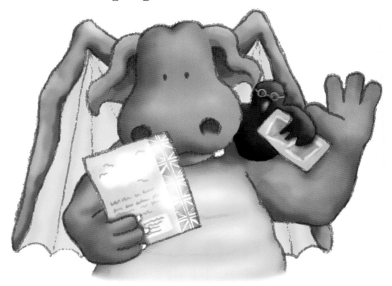

"Right," said Tiberius. "Now we are all here, let's decide where we will go for our day out. Any ideas?"

"Yes!" they all said in unison.

"One at a time," said Tiberius. "I expect you will all want to go somewhere different."

"Well, I've got a brochure of where I'd like to go," said Sneaky Cat.

"So have I," said Croaky Crow.

"And I've been to the travel agent," said Drag proudly, "and he has given me a very good idea and a brochure."

"Who is going to speak first?" asked Tiberius.

"Not me," said Sneaky Cat.

"Nor me," said Croaky Crow.

"Mine is the best idea," said Drag, "so I must be last."

"Oh dear!" Tiberius exclaimed. "Someone has to go first."

"Not really," said Croaky Crow. "How about if we all turn our brochures over at the same time and then everyone will see where we have each chosen at the same time."

"What a good idea," said Tiberius. "I'll count to three then you all turn them over. One, two, threeeee."

As they turned their brochures over, they all started to laugh.

"I don't believe this," said Tiberius.

"You've all chosen the same place. It's just as well I would like to go there, too!"

Sneaky Cat's brochure was called 'A day out in London'. Croaky Crow's was 'An excursion to London'. And Drag had brought 'Things to see in London'.

"London it is, then!" said Tiberius.

They all nodded in agreement.

"But when shall we go?" asked Croaky Crow.

"As soon as possible," said Tiberius. "I will try to book train tickets for next Friday and we can go early in the morning. I can arrange for Sir Patrick to give us a lift to the station. I'm sure he won't mind and we can all meet here at 9 o'clock."

Everybody agreed.

Sir Patrick was their friend who lived at the Castle with his daughter, Georgina.

"I think that will be alright," said Croaky with a smile on his face, "but I usually fly everywhere."

Friday morning soon came and Sneaky Cat, Croaky Crow and Drag all arrived at half past eight as none of them wanted to be late.

Tiberius made them all a drink while they waited for Sir Patrick to arrive. He was picking them up at 9 o'clock as the train was due to leave the station at 9.30.

"What shall we go to see first?" asked Drag. "I'd like to see Buckingham Palace and all the soldiers."

"I don't mind where we go," said Sneaky Cat, "as long as it's not high up. You know I don't like heights."

"Let's wait until we get there," said Tiberius, "and we will try to fit in as much as we can."

It was now five minutes past nine and there was no sign of Sir Patrick. "I wonder what's happened to him," said Drag.

"Perhaps it was a mistake to ask him," said Tiberius, "especially after what happened to his car when it broke down on the way to the picnic."

At ten past nine Sir Patrick still hadn't arrived.

By quarter past nine they were becoming very worried. Neither Sir Patrick nor his car were anywhere in sight.

They all went down to Tiberius' gate to look for him, but no-one was there.

"Oh dear. The train leaves the station in fifteen minutes. Unless something happens soon we will miss the train," moaned Drag.

Then something DID happen.

The village fire engine came hurtling around the corner and screeched to a stop in front of them. Tiberius and his friends were amazed.

"Hop on board," said the fire chief. "Sir Patrick says I've got to get you to the station for half past nine."

"What's happened to Sir Patrick?" asked Tiberius with a worried look on his face.

"We've just had to rescue him," said the fire chief. "He was stuck in a ditch in his car."

"Oh no!" said Tiberius.

"He was going round a corner when the steering wheel came off in his hands and he just went straight on instead of round the corner. You know what his car is like! He said he was on his way here to collect you and take you to the station and it was very important. We pulled him out of the ditch, then we volunteered to help. And here we are!"

"Hurry up and climb on board. We haven't got much time!"

They all clambered aboard the fire engine.

The fireman rang the bell and they raced through the streets. All the cars moved out of the way, thinking that the fire engine was on its way to a fire!

The fire engine soon arrived at the station.

"Thank you so much," said Tiberius. "You make an extremely useful taxi."

The station master saw them rushing on to the platform. It was 9.29!

"Could you stop a minute please?" asked Tiberius. "My friends haven't seen this before."

"Who's that standing on the top of that tall column?" asked Drag.

"I don't know and I'm not going to find out," said Sneaky Cat.

"That," said Tiberius very knowledgeably, "is Lord Nelson. He stands at the top of the column."

"How does he get his food?" asked Drag.

"Don't be silly," said Tiberius, "it's a statue. He's made of stone."

"Look at all those pigeons," said Croaky Crow. "I wonder if I know any of them?"

He was just about to get out of the cab when Tiberius stopped him.

"I don't think we have time at the moment, Croaky. We must get on to the Eye"

"Alright, alright," said Croaky looking very disappointed.

The taxi sped off again to its next port of call, the London Eye.

It pulled up near the big wheel. Tiberius paid the taxi driver and they all got out.

"WOW!" said Drag. "This IS impressive!"

"When you get to the top you can see all over London and if you go when it's dark it is very pretty and quite spectacular," said Tiberius.

"I'm not very impressed," said Croaky Crow with a little laugh. "I can see London from that height any time I like without going in a little pod."

"By the way," said Tiberius, "where is Sneaky Cat?"

They all looked round, but there was no sign of him.

They walked past the queue of people waiting to go on the London Eye, but couldn't see him anywhere.

They went to the hot dog stand. He wasn't there either.

They even went into the gift shop, but there was no sign of him there.

"Are you sure he came with us?" asked Drag.

"Yes, I'm sure," said Tiberius. "I saw him get out of the taxi. But where is he now?"

"What are we going to do?" asked Drag.

"I don't know," said Tiberius, "but I don't think he can have gone too far away. I am sure he will be back in a minute."

Just then they heard a very loud "MEOW, MEOW, MEOW! Help! Help! Help! Send for the fire brigade."

"I know that voice," said Tiberius.

"It's Sneaky Cat! And by the sound of his voice I can guess where he is."

They all looked upwards at the Eye. There, nearly at the top, was Sneaky Cat in one of the pods, jumping up and down.

"Help! Help! Get me down!"

"However did he get up there?" asked Croaky Crow. "Perhaps I should fly up there and try to calm him down. I must say, this is becoming a habit having to rescue Sneaky from high places."

Croaky Crow flew up to the pod and landed on its roof.

"Hi, Sneaky," said Croaky, trying not
to laugh. "How did you get in there?"

"I'm sorry I am a liability," said Sneaky Cat.
"You were all looking at the Eye and I
thought you might take a ride on it. I saw
what I thought was a cabin and I crept into a
corner of it to keep out of the way. Now look
what's happened. I fell asleep and woke up
right up here."

"Help! Help! Send for the fire brigade."

"Don't panic," said Croaky Crow. "We don't need the fire brigade. The wheel goes round slowly and it will take you back to the bottom. Just look at the wonderful view."

"You might like views from this height, Croaky, but I don't," said Sneaky. "Help!"

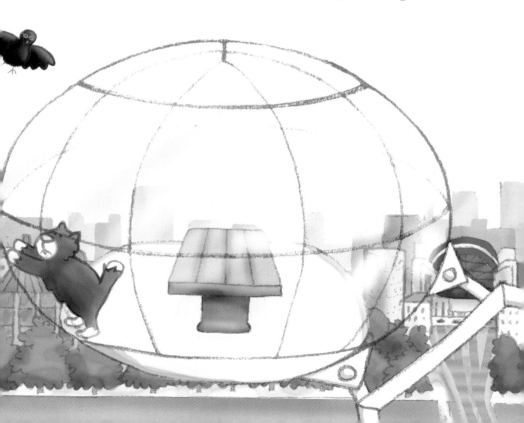

"It only moves very slowly, but don't worry, I'll stay here until we get to the bottom."

When Sneaky Cat eventually got to the ground again, he staggered out of the pod.

"Oh, Tiberius," Sneaky Cat said. "Do keep an eye on me, I am hopeless."

"That's enough excitement here," said Drag. "Let's get off to the Tower of London."

They all had a last look up at the Eye and some of them wished that they had been on it. Sneaky wished he hadn't.

"The Tower of London next," said Tiberius, "but this time we will go by bus."

The four friends found a bus stop and waited for the next bus to come. They looked for one saying 'Tower of London' on the front.

Eventually one came and they all climbed aboard.

The conductor rang the bell and the bus zoomed down the bus lane to the Tower.

When they first saw the Tower, Drag said, "This is almost like Sir Patrick's castle, except this is much bigger."

"It does look like a castle," said Croaky Crow. "Look at all those ravens. I think my cousin must be here somewhere."

"Now be careful all of you," said Tiberius with a smile. "They have dungeons here. If you misbehave, you might be put in one."

They were not sure whether Tiberius was teasing them or not, but Sneaky Cat said he would be very careful.

They walked around and saw the Beefeaters marching.

Drag was so
impressed that
he had his picture
taken standing
next to one.

They saw the
Crown Jewels
and looked over the
wall at Tower Bridge.

Time passed very quickly and Tiberius then
decided it was time to go to Buckingham
Palace.

"To see the Queen?" asked Drag.

"I don't think she will be there," said Sneaky
Cat, "but we might be lucky."

"We lost Sneaky Cat at the Eye. If everybody is here, we can set off for the Palace," said Tiberius. "I'll call out your names."

"Drag!"

"Here," said Drag.

"Sneaky Cat!"

"Here," said Sneaky Cat.

"Croaky Crow!"

But then there was only silence.

"Oh no! Where's Croaky Crow?" asked Tiberius. "Now HE has disappeared."

"Do yo   search
party?   many
peopl

"Yes,   in different
place   n minutes."

So off they all set in different directions.
Sneaky Cat went right and Tiberius went left.
Drag just looked around.

'I know,' thought Drag. 'I'll ask a policeman.
He might be able to help.'

There was a very
large policeman
standing at the gate.
Drag went up to the
policeman and smiled.

"Excuse me," he said, "I am looking for my friend, Croaky Crow. He is a black bird with big glasses. Have you seen him?"

The policeman laughed. "Oh dear," he said. "There are so many birds about today. I don't know. Just look at that crowd of ravens over there."

Drag looked over by the Tower wall. There seemed to be hundreds of ravens all very excitedly talking to another bird.

"Goodness me," he said to himself. "The other bird is Croaky!"

Drag walked slowly over to him. "We've been looking for you," he said. "We thought you'd been put in the dungeon."

"Sorry," said Croaky, "but I've just met three of my cousins. I haven't seen them for years."

Then the ravens all started talking at the same time again.

"Sorry, I must go. It's been lovely to see you all," said Croaky. "We only have one day here in London. Perhaps I'll come back some other time."

With that he waved goodbye and went back with Drag to find Sneaky Cat and Tiberius.

"Thank goodness we've found you," said Tiberius. "I think we may just have time now to get something to eat and stop and see Big Ben on the way to the Palace."

"Big Ben? Do I know him?" asked Drag.

"Don't be silly," said Tiberius. "Big Ben is the name of the bell in the clock on the Houses of Parliament, but everyone calls the clock Big Ben as well. We can go by boat up the river to Westminster, see Big Ben and then go on to the Palace."

The four bought some sandwiches and then stepped aboard a boat at Tower Bridge and set off up the river. Croaky Crow sat right at the back. He enjoyed sitting on the flagpole at the back of the boat eating his cheese sandwich.

"I feel just like a seagull," he said.

"As long as you haven't got any more cousins to surprise you, that's fine," said Tiberius.

They arrived at Westminster and looked up at Big Ben. The clock was just striking four o'clock.
BONG! BONG! BONG! BONG!

"That's very loud," said Sneaky Cat and put his paws over his ears. "I'm glad we won't be here when it strikes twelve!"

They had only been there for a few minutes when Tiberius suggested they should move on to Buckingham Palace.

Drag said they had been on a train, a taxi, a bus and a boat, so they must go on a tube train.

Sneaky Cat, Drag and Tiberius decided to go by tube, but Croaky said that it would be quicker for him to fly and he would meet them at the gates of the Palace.

When they all arrived there were lots of people there.

"This is exciting," said Sneaky Cat. "What's happening?"

"Oh," said Tiberius, being very knowledgeable again, "everyone has come to see if they can see the Queen."

"Is the Queen at home?" asked Sneaky Cat.

"Yes, I think so," said Tiberius. "You can see the flag flying at the top of the flagpole."

"I'll fly past some of the windows to see if I can spot her," said Croaky Crow. "I hope I won't get into trouble."

"If you are going to do that, fly very quickly," said Tiberius, putting his hands over his eyes.

"OK," said Croaky and flew across the front of the Palace almost as fast as a jet plane.

"Did you see anything?" asked Drag when Croaky got back.

"Yes, I think so," said Croaky. "The Queen's crown was hanging up behind the door in her bedroom, so she must be in the Palace."

"Are you sure?" asked Tiberius.

"Positive," said Croaky Crow with a grin.

They waited and they waited but she did not appear. They were quite disappointed not to see the Queen.

"Now, before we go home," said Tiberius, "we should buy a souvenir of our day out in London."

They all went to a gift shop and bought a present for themselves. Then they got on a bus which took them straight to the station.

The station master saw them coming and recognised Drag. "Have you had a nice day?" he asked.

"It was wonderful!" said Drag.

"And we have had a great time, too," said the others. "We've seen everything."

"Your train's on platform 4," said the station master, "and it leaves in ten minutes, so you have plenty of time. Enjoy the trip home!"

They couldn't stop talking about their day out in London and the journey seemed to go very quickly. When the train pulled into the station it was already quite late. In fact it was nearly ten o'clock.

"I don't suppose the fire engine will be here," said Drag.

"No, I don't think so," said Tiberius as they

got off the train.

"Hi there. You're a bit late back," a voice called from the end of the platform.

"Look who it is!" said Drag. "It's Sir Patrick."

"I'm sorry that I let you down this morning, but I thought I would make up for it by meeting you off the train," said Sir Patrick with a big smile on his face.

"How nice of you," said Tiberius, "but are you sure nothing will fall off the car this time?"

"I hope not!" said Sir Patrick.

They all laughed and Sir Patrick drove them home after a very, very happy day.